The Sleeping Beauty

Illustrations by J. L. MACIAS S.

Retold by JANE CARRUTH

Once upon a time there lived a King and Queen who longed, with all their hearts, for a child of their own.

After many years, and to their great joy, the Queen gave birth to a beautiful baby girl. All the people rejoiced with them.

"We must invite all our friends to the Christening Party," said the Queen. "And we must invite all the fairies."

Alas, the King forgot to send an invitation to one of the oldest and most important fairies in the land and so he had no special present made for her.

The fairies who came to the Christening bestowed upon the baby many wonderful gifts. Beauty and grace and intelligence would all be hers as she grew up. Then, suddenly, the oldest fairy in the land appeared, dressed in black and with a face twisted in rage. "I, too, have a gift for the royal baby!" she screamed. "She will die from the prick of a spindle when she is fifteen years old!" And she laughed loudly.

Now the youngest of the fairies had not yet bestowed her gift on the little Princess.

"Be of good heart," she told the horrified King and Queen. "The child will not die. She will fall into a deep sleep which will last one hundred years, and then a king's son shall wake her." But the royal parents could not be comforted and the King said that every spindle in the land must be burned. Any person caught using a spinning wheel would be put to death.

Years passed and the Princess grew into a beautiful young girl, greatly loved by all who knew her. On her fifteenth birthday her parents took her to their castle in the country, where she was free to walk and play in the gardens, and ride her pony along country lanes.

One day, the Princess set out to explore all the small rooms at the very top of the castle. In one, she came upon an old woman, busy spinning. "Let me try, good mother!" she cried.

Now the old woman had not heard of the wicked fairy's curse or even that the King had a daughter. "Take it then, my pretty child," she said, handing her spindle to the Princess. Almost at once the girl felt a sharp prick and, with a small cry, she fell to the ground and lay as if dead. Terrified, the old woman rushed from her turret room, shouting for help.

Sadly, the King and Queen told their servants to carry the Princess to her bed-chamber. Then a strange thing happened.

All who were in the castle that day fell into a deep sleep. Even the cats and dogs and the little doves went to sleep.

This was the work of the youngest fairy, who came to the castle in her chariot drawn by dragons. So powerful was her magic that even the cook fell asleep in the very act of tasting the soup, and the jesters in the middle of telling jokes! One hundred years passed and all around the castle had grown a thick hedge of briars and thorns.

One day, a king's son was hunting in the forest and when he heard the story from an old woodcutter of the Sleeping Beauty in the strange, silent castle, he made up his mind to cut through the thick hedge and break into the castle so that he might find out for himself if the story was true.

The Prince drew his sword, but it was not needed, for a path appeared and he had only to follow it to reach the castle gates.

All was still and silent as the young Prince began his search for
the Sleeping Beauty. He came upon her at last, lying on a bed of
silver, her golden hair spread about her shoulders. And so lovely
was she that the Prince lost his heart to her.

"So the story of the Sleeping Beauty is true," he said to himself,
as he stood gazing at her. "How wonderfully beautiful she is!"
Slowly, he approached the bed. Then he bent down and gently
kissed the Princess. At the touch of his lips, she opened her eyes,
and the sleeping castle came to bustling life.

The Princess, on waking, knew that she too had found her true love and the very next day they were married. So beautiful did she look on her Wedding Day that the Prince did not even notice that her wedding gown was one hundred years out of fashion!

Published in United States and simultaneously in Canada by Joshua Morris, I
431 Post Road East, Westport, CT 068
Printed in Belgi